Harry and his family were in the
garden trying to keep cool. But Harry
was fed up.

"Can't we play a game?" he said.
"No," said his mum. "It's too hot, and
I'm too busy reading."

"No," yawned his dad. "It's too hot,
and I'm too busy sleeping."

"No," said his big sister. "It's too hot, and I'm too busy listening to my music."

But Harry still wanted to play a game.

He went back into the house, peeled a big juicy orange, and had a think. Then he put on his face mask and flippers and flip-flapped outside to his mum.

"If you played a game of deep-sea diving with me," he said, "I would give you this big juicy orange."

And he held up the orange, tripped over his flippers, and squished juice right in his mum's ear.

"Ow! Don't do that, Harry," said his mum. "Look at the mess you've made."

Harry made a scowly face. His mum was no fun at all.

But he still wanted to play a game.
He went back into the house,
unwrapped a big chocolate ice cream,
and had a think.

Then he put on his wrist bands, took his tennis racquet, and flip-flapped outside to his dad.

"If you played a game of deep-sea diving or tennis with me," he said, "I would give you this big chocolate ice cream."

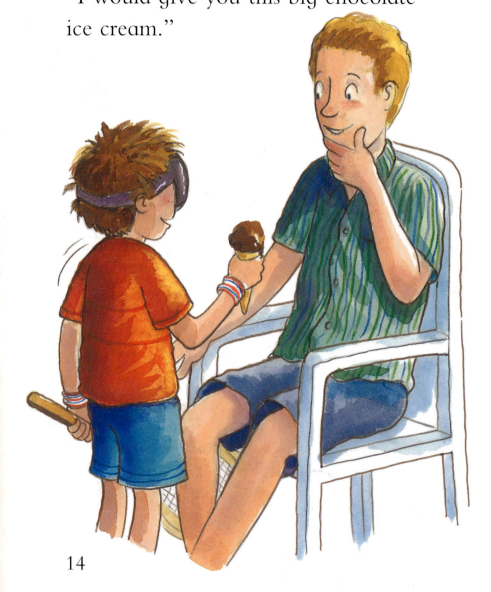

And he held out the ice cream, tripped
over his flippers and stuck the ice cream
right up his dad's nose.

15

"Ow! Ow! Don't do that, Harry!"
yelled his dad. "Look at the mess
you've made."

Harry made another scowly face.
His dad was no fun at all.

But he still wanted to play a game.
He went back into the house, filled up
a big glass with ice and lemonade, and
had a think.

Then he put on an old straw hat, picked up his fishing net, and flip-flapped outside to his big sister.

His big sister had on her headphones, so Harry lifted one off and yelled in her ear.

"If you played a game of deep-sea diving or tennis or fishing with me," he said, "I would give you some of this ice-cold lemonade."

And he held out the ice-cold lemonade,
tripped over his flippers and poured it
all over his sister's bare tum.

"Ow! Ow! Ow!" yelled his sister.
"Don't do that, Harry. Look at the
mess you've made."

Harry made his best scowly face ever.
His sister was no fun at all.

By now he was feeling very hot, dressed
in all the play things. Then he spied the
garden hose.

"I could play a game with that," he said. "That would keep me cool."

He picked up the garden hose and turned it full on. It made a lovely whooshing noise.

"Don't do that, Harry!" yelled his family. "Look at the mess—"

"What?" said Harry, and turned round
with the hose and WHOOOOOOOSH
soaked them all.

"Owwwwwwwwwww!" yelled his
dripping family. "Just wait till we get
you!" And they chased Harry round
and round the garden.

Harry made a huge smiley face. "This is a great game," he cried. "Why didn't you tell me you wanted to play chases!"

Harry's family were good fun after all, and, when they got too hot chasing him, he knew EXACTLY how to cool them down!